RETURN TO BURKE COUNTY

INSPIRED BY A TRUE STORY

RE LEWIS

RETURN TO BURKE COUNTY

INSPIRED BY A TRUE STORY

Written by RE LEWIS
https://RELEWIS.us

CONTENTS

INTRODUCTION

Roby Martin had just lost the love of his young life. Without Anna, he had no family and no reason to return home to Burke County. But Roby was wrong. When the North Carolina Sheriff arrested him as he addressed the General Assembly in Kentucky, Roby was not surprised that it was for murder.

A national figure in politics arrested for a murder twenty-five years ago, one might think people would understand and possibly forgive an accidental death in the post-civil war era of 1867. But the extraordinary attention was not about the murder of Cal Porter; it was about the details and the moral complexity of the second charge against him. That charge made the entire South focus on the outcome of the murder trial of Roby Martin.

* * *

Author RE LEWIS spent nearly his entire adult life in the mountains. Born and raised in the South, Lewis didn't just study the people and history of the deep south; he lived it with the love, loss, sacrifice, and dedication of the truest native southerners.

The no-nonsense understanding of real-life events and the honest and staunch morality of "Mountain Justice" is tested in 1892 and always found in what the Appalachian natives call "the hills." The Roby Martin story is inspired by actual events and is a mirror of mountain justice today. Many names have been changed, but the extraordinary events are authentic.

Finding yourself and your loved ones in this story will be easy. But will you like what you discover?

RETURN TO BURKE COUNTY

1892

The wagon ruts were deeper than a well bucket and filled with mud from the heavy April rain. The aging wagon was weakened from the aggressive undertaking, creaking and groaning with each turn of the wheels. It was slow going, the axel grinding plainly a sign of trouble. April snow, at this altitude in the Blue Ridge, would have been typical enough. Still, the heavy rain was more damaging to the mountain roads. The air felt cold enough for snow, but the piercing rain proved that spring was on its way, although it was not yet kind enough to show its warmer face. As more of the day passed, the trail was rapidly becoming treacherous.

Shackled, wet, shivering, bearded, and bruised, Roby Martin was now quiet after six days of pressing the Sheriff for answers. He had spent these days trying to find out why

1

the Burke County Sheriff was taking him back to the County seat of Morganton for trial. His persistent questioning was finally met with a rifle stock across the face, and a few hours of missing memory, before waking with a new bruise flowering on his temple.

All Roby knew was that he was facing trial for murder, which he understood. This, in itself, was not at all surprising. There was another charge on his head, though, one that he was aware of being fact but hadn't yet been explained to him. This confused Martin. Why the secrecy? What could possibly be so much worse than murder? What was so terrible that the Sheriff didn't want to talk about it with the prisoner whom he had traveled more than two hundred miles to arrest?

Roby did know that in 1867, twenty-five years earlier, someone had visited his cabin. More specifically, they had seen his wife, Anna, while she was alone. He knew it had been earlier in the day and that the surprise visitor had been Cal Porter - the only son of Burke County's wealthiest family. Past that, his knowledge was limited to what Anna had told him about the encounter. Everyone thought this encounter led to Cal Porter's death at the hands of Roby Martin.

ANNA

1867

*A*nna Pruitt Martin, Roby's childhood neighbor, sweetheart, and now his young bride of two perfect years, was preparing their artfully crafted cabin for his arrival. Returning from the hunt, he would haul in his kills, and as always, they would work together to butcher and preserve the day's game.

Weekends were spent hunting and fishing, while on weekdays, Roby worked as a skilled carpenter and craftsman for the Porter family lumber mill. Roby would also take on special projects for other families, builders, and businesses whenever he could. Burke County was struggling terribly after the prolonged war. Still, his services were valuable, so business was usually quite good.

Anna was busy cleaning the skillet. As she greased it carefully in preparation for the venison she was sure would be arriving, when she heard the familiar sound of an approaching rider. Assuming, reasonably so, that it was Roby on his way back from the hunt, she rushed over to the door. Her eyes, a soft, eager green, squinted suspiciously at the rider. Her uneven, engaging smile disappeared when she discovered It wasn't Roby. Anna pushed a flurry of auburn locks away from her face as he approached, trying to hide her disappointment.

"Oh," she said, "Mr. Porter, I thought you were Roby."

"So, he's not here?" Cal said in mock surprise.

Cal Porter was a bold man on a regular day but was emboldened still by his family fortune. Over the years, he had taken a particular liking to Anna, despite them both being married. It annoyed him completely that Roby had won her heart instead.

Cal knew Roby would be hunting, as he usually did on Saturday morning from before dawn until early afternoon. Aside from his regular business dealings, hunting was the best way for Roby to earn money.

"You know he's not here, Cal. You always know he's not here. What do you want this day?"

"Same thing I always want, Anna. I want to know why you're wastin' time with that…."

Cal paused as if searching for the perfect word to describe his nemesis but always returned with the same word describing his disdain for people of less stature than himself.

"Hireling!" Cal spits from his mouth.

The words were venom from his tongue, but it didn't bother her anymore in that very same tone. Anna had stopped thinking less of Cal every time he spoke. She couldn't think less of him because she didn't think of him at all.

Cal slid from his horse, landing dizzily on the ground. From the porch, Anna could see his cheeks flushed in the familiar tint of having "tipped the jug" too often.

He patted his horse momentarily and then, without warning, lurched forward up the steps to throw his outstretched arms around Anna. Still holding the partially-greased skillet in her hand, Anna quickly brandished it. Cal's sudden advance was met with the underside of an iron skillet square atop his forehead. He dropped like a sack of flour and tumbled down the steps faster than he had climbed them. Cal landed in a crumpled heap at the foot of his horse. Violently spooked, his mare bolted toward the Porter estate and quickly raced out of sight.

"A bit early in the day to be in the shine, isn't it, Cal?" Anna called sternly, peering down at him from the top of the steps.

"You better get started, Cal. It's going to be a long walk home."

"That's not funny, Anna," Cal retorted, somehow managing to stumble upward onto his feet. "Damn, that hurt."

"Try anything like that again, Mr. Porter, and I'll show you some real and proper hurt."

"I'll be needin' your horse then. You scared mine off."

"You'll be gettin' nothing from me besides another lick with this skillet if you don't start walking!"

"But," stammered Cal, obviously searching for reasons to stay or convince that horse out of her.

"Listen. It'll be dark 'fore I get home, and… well, there's mountain lions out there! Big un's!"

"Yeah, but it's the black bears you got to worry about." Anna grinned. "You can borrow my skillet if you like. If it can drop a drunk bastard four steps, it might be good against a bear, too."

Cal glared at her. "Fine. Maybe I'll get me 'nother mill-hand too."

"You better get going!" she added, waving. "If Roby sees you here… well, you don't want to be here to find out."

Walking considerably slower than normal, Cal began limping east towards the Mill and his home. With a bruised ego, a twisted ankle from the fall, and a massive headache, Cal gingerly felt the knot that had already begun to resemble a spike horn on his forehead. He was still mumbling to himself and glancing back in the direction of Anna when the sun crested Timber Ridge and began its descent into the gorge.

SHARING

1867

*H*ours after Cal Porter disappeared down the forest trail, limping and staggering like a wounded deer, Roby emerged from the forest with a large buck across his horse's flank. He had accompanied his father on such hunts since he was old enough to hold onto his father's waist. He had also become a hunter and marksman, second to no one in the mountains.

Roby often remembered when he and his father would spend the day hunting. He recalled the first time they tracked a rafter of turkey, set a blind, and called them in. Roby and his father watched, peeking from under a laurel bough, as six turkeys cautiously approached the pair of hunters. The rhododendron and Laurel blooms in late spring contrasted against the green flora for excellent camouflage.

"Here they come, Roby. Which one should we take?" Martin whispered.

"There, That one. The big one!" Roby pointed with his finger touching the laurel, barely containing his excitement. The turkey turned and started away until a single guttural call from Martin's throat recalled their interest and brought them slowly back in the direction of Roby.

"Shhh, they'll hear you. That's a hen, the mama. Who will take care of the Jakes and the Jennies if we take the mama?

"Oh, yeah. How 'bout that one with the long beard?" Roby looked into his father's eyes for approval.

"That's a good choice, son." Martin whispered, "He's the oldest and maybe the weakest now. There's another Tom over there with a beard, just not as long. He's younger and maybe stronger."

"Take aim slowly. When you are calm, exhale and pull the trigger." Martin said slowly, quietly.

A sharp crack, a glory of smoke, and a flurry of feathers produced a 35lb Tom that Roby would carry back to his home with the prideful grin of a successful provider.

"Well, Roby, I do believe that's the biggest turkey I've ever seen!" His mother said to Roby the way a mother does when she's encouraged by her husband's smile and her son's pride.

On the ride home long ago, Martin explained to his son, "Today, we put food on the table. We did it without weakening the family of turkey. They're strong now, and they'll continue to grow even stronger. Living with the forest's creatures that will sustain us is up to us. We must allow them to thrive too."

* * *

The Large buck Roby had taken this Saturday morning was now field-dressed and wrapped but not butchered. Roby and Anna would carefully perform this task together. Unromantic as this may seem for most, the two found some closeness in it. Each bit of meat, prepared by their own hands and sold, was a step closer to their goal. Roby's family had owned this land before the war, and as the earnings stacked up, it became more and more realistic of a pursuit to pay the taxes that would reclaim it.

As they finished the cabin and paid the new taxes, the land would belong to the Martins again. The post-war Governor's taxing of land assets was a crushing debt but a burden that landowners took seriously. Since Anna and Roby wanted to raise a family, this land was crucial in their plans. Anna would wrap the choicest cuts to sell, while Roby would salt the stores and work the hides. They would talk and laugh together, enjoying the stories of their day.

Anna told Roby about Cal Porter's visit. They were bent over laughing, nearly to tears, as she described his tumble from the stairs, the knot on his head, and watching him limping into the distance talking to himself. While Anna felt somewhat sorry for Cal, Roby knew he got what he deserved and got off lightly because Anna had a pistol and knew how to use it well.

In the early evening, after finishing the preparation of the game, Roby and Anna would take the 100-yard walk together to the natural spring nearby the cabin. There, appearing to rise to the surface in the roots of a large maple, the spring trickled lightly down the hill like a waterfall, landing on an edged platform Roby had constructed. The platform was a flat surface that captured and pooled the crystalline water on top. The sun shined on the fire-blackened oakwood roof and warmed the shallow pool. It produced a satisfying curtain of warm water for bathing after a long day's work. Anna and Roby looked forward to this time for many reasons. It was an opportunity to wash clothes, to relax, and to share their day and each other's warmth. Today, they found the opportunity to embrace and share their love, their dreams, and their need for each other.

Roby asked, "Did you bring your skillet?"

Confused, Anna asked, "No, why would I…."

Roby grabbed Anna and dragged her, laughing, into the standing pool created by the waterfall.

They laughed, talked, and they embraced. Roby never tired of looking into Anna's green eyes.

Holding hands on their way back to the cabin was a sign of their need to share each other's touch. Anna would look Roby in the eyes and run her hand up Roby's sleeve. Roby smiles at her to say, "You're stretching my shirt…." Then they would steal the moment together as private.

Late evenings in the cabin, Anna would study her father's medical books and journals by lamplight. She would often talk to Roby across the room as he whittled away at his latest project. Anna helped her father often, working as a nurse in his Burke County practice. These nights were crucial to ensuring all her medical knowledge was up to her father's expectations. She had grown up with a high value on education, born to a family of doctors.

Having lost his parents during the war, then serving in the last year of the war - much younger than expected - Roby could not focus on education. He respected higher education, but it had been necessary for him to work, learn a trade, and fight. Life, for Roby, had taken priority over his schooling – a much too typical path for young men in the mountains. Few people in the area had the luxury of spending the day in a schoolhouse poring over books instead of doing backbreaking physical labor in the surrounding mountains and townships. Men had to work the fields, the mills, and the stills.

Before he turned twenty, Roby was already a masterful carpenter and respected for his craftsmanship and considerable work ethic. Able to earn and save his money, he was happy to be on his way to becoming the property owner and provider he knew Anna deserved. His love and respect for the woman he married were apparent in how he treated her.

Anna and Roby shared everything, valuing their time together more than most, with hunting being one of the few exceptions. Anna had never gotten used to taking the lives of

God's creatures. She wanted nothing more than to just spend her life with Roby. It was clear to everyone that met them that they loved and respected each other to an almost overly modern interrelation. Anna had an equal say in the decisions of their household business. They took on life's challenges as a team. As long as they were together, nothing would get in their way.

Although committed to studying her father's medical books, Anna momentarily drifts back to a time in her childhood when her father asked her what she wanted to be. Would she be a teacher? A doctor? A lawyer... Uh, no, not a lawyer – Dr. Pruitt would never allow that. But while every option would be possible, being a doctor was always the path that appealed to her most. A lofty goal for a woman in 1860, talent was the accurate benchmark, and Anna was overly qualified. She watched and studied her father's actions and deeds. She saw him as an honorable and compassionate man that would run to tend to the needs of families, friends, and strangers. To Anna, there was nothing as noble and selfless as that. Her parents adored her and watched her grow to be a wise and compassionate woman by letting her make decisions on her own behalf.

Born into a family inclined to medicine, one might think she was pressed into following the family trade. Still, the Pruitts were careful to encourage Anna to make her own decisions about her path. It was not a surprise that Anna was inclined to follow that lead. Her flair for helping people and tending to their pain became her drive.

One day, she just knew it would happen. The first time she followed her father to the hospital to observe, and to satisfy her curiosity, the atmosphere was uncomfortable because the smell of sickness permeated the air. The complaining and crying proved unsettling for her. Still, she found a young boy, a friend, writhing in pain, lying on his belly on a table in the large examination room. It was her friend Lewis Redmond.

Lewis had been working in a corn field that morning when he disturbed a nest of poisonous Pack Saddles in the silk of a corn stalk. A handful of the poisonous caterpillar-like devils fell on his back and down his soaked cotton shirt. Several were trapped beneath his shirt on his bare skin.

Pack Saddles have dozens of hair-like stingers that create a fiery sting only equaled by yellow jackets. There appeared to be almost a hundred stings on Lewis's back; one by one, the stingers had to be removed. A simple enough process or "operation," as Dr. Pruitt would describe it to Anna, she was given the task of removing each one of the stingers.

Inspecting the acorn-sized welts on Lewis's back, she could clearly see the light-colored stinger rising out of the center. Lewis was feeling sick and starting to swell all over - his breathing was becoming labored. Nobody had to tell Anna to hurry.

By removing the stingers, each one offered Lewis a measure of relief. With each of the eighty stingers she pulled, Anna felt more emboldened. Removing all of the stingers resulted in great relief to Lewis, and eighty times, Anna felt a fantastic sense of accomplishment and satisfaction seeing her friend begin to relax and rest. There was no question that Anna would now follow the family tradition. It was not, however, because of family tradition. This was a personal sense of accomplishment, service, and empowerment. One could call it an epiphany for Anna, but she called it a blessing.

Anna flipped thru the pages of her medical book indecisively. Looking up at Roby, who was looking intently at her, Roby said, "Are you good?"

"Yes, I was thinking about that time I pulled stingers out of Lewis's back. That was the day I knew what I wanted to do forever."

It was also the day Lewis Redmond knew what he didn't want to do ever again.

SUNDAY

1866

*S*unday mornings brought an opportunity to ride into town for Church and to take fresh game to the butcher. Roby would also sell his handmade furniture at the general store. More than anything, it was a chance to pay a visit to Anna's family.

Protective yet supportive, Anna's family had grown to appreciate and respect Roby Martin in spite of their initial reservations. It had been doubtful whether or not the mill-hand would be able to provide the quality of life that a doctor's daughter was raised to enjoy.

Anna would tell her parents, "Roby treats me with respect, and he loves me just as you do. Roby's a good man. A man of character with a good plan to take care of our family. He doesn't need to be a doctor. He owns property, and he will take care of us just fine. Don't worry about Roby, and don't worry about me."

That simple declaration would well end any discussion they wanted to have about the prospect of having Roby Martin as a son-in-law. Anna made it clear that her mind was settled, so their choice was a life with him or a life without her.

The Church was another story. Anna was strong in her faith and active in the Church the way any young woman would be. Roby was not so comfortable with his involvement. There was the constant prying, the pressure to give his testimony, the confessions, and the pressure of the Church officers to become more involved.

Although Roby had grown up in the Church, he had lost his mother early and then his father to the war - adding to that the nightmares he had experienced himself, it was plain to say he had just cause to be suspicious of the faith and motives of men. Roby would not even entertain the idea of sharing his experiences and doubts with those he did not fully trust. Still, one of Roby's fondest memories of his mother and father was attending Church together every Sunday. All of the Burke County families would gather and enjoy the fellowship of a simpler time, and it was there that he first met and soon grew to love Anna Pruitt, the only daughter of the Burke County doctor James Pruitt.

The families would always seem to find each other because they shared the common gift of a light-hearted, albeit mordant, sense of humor. Except for their dislike of politicians, politics, and people that take advantage of the kindness of others, their warmth and humor were enjoyed by most of the congregation and other Burke County families.

Roby would think back at what seemed a lifetime ago when, on a regular Sunday with everyone chatting, Jacob Small, the county solicitor, sidled up and joined the conversation. No one seemed to appreciate Small's presence. He had the unfortunate curse of souring any conversation merely by being a contrary know-it-all and standing there surveying the others like he was glaring directly into their souls and finding them wanting. If Robert Martin had heard, "Well, actually, my good man..." followed by his uninformed opinion one more time, the entire congregation would have witnessed an unexpected baptism in the holy water of the Yadkin River.

Upon Small's apparition, one which would have been well-accompanied by a puff of smoke, Robert Martin was quick to direct the conversation to fishing for trout. He and Dr. Pruitt would, in the summer, spend what little free time they could find fishing the French Broad River for brook trout, and there was plenty of common ground to be found there. The lawyer, however, didn't care for nature – a rare trait for someone in the beautiful Appalachian Mountains - and so, Small would bid his farewell as quickly as he had appeared, tipping his hat to the ladies and moving on to find conversation more to his liking.

"What was it, do you think, that made him leave this

time?" Roby remembered Dr. Pruitt asking, stifling a smile. "The thought of touching a fish?"

"Ah, he shutters to think of fishing. Small doesn't realize he would be right at home with the snakes and horseflies. He must worry the fish will mistake him for bait." Robert snickered.

His head turned to watch Small make his way across the room, moving from group to group like a ghost, as his pale skin suggested, hovering over their shoulders.

"Don't you dare take after your fathers now, you hear?" Mrs. Pruitt interrupted, pointing a stern finger at Roby and Anna. "It is Sunday, after all, and it is not the time to be unkind." Her piercing glance at Captain Martin and Dr. Pruitt made the entire group take a break of silence and redirect their conversation.

"So, Doc, can you get away for some fly fishing in the mornin'?" brought the entire group to the verge of tearful laughter.

Except for Mrs. Pruitt, of course...

THE WAR

1865

The war had been raging for nearly four years when Roby set out to find his father. It had been too long. In spite of Anna's protests, Roby knew it was something that had to be done. He had not heard from his father in over a year and knew the only way to find out what had happened to him was to follow the fight. Roby looked and carried himself mature for his age, but by this time, the Confederate army was accepting anyone who could hold a rifle – especially so for a marksman of Roby's talent. In the summer of 1865, it didn't really matter how old he was.

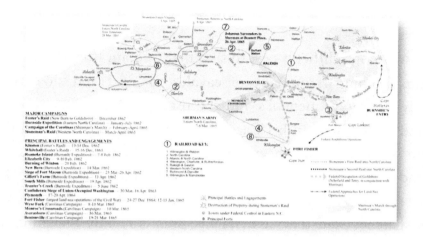

Anna had only two demands; the first being that Roby returns home safely, and the second was that he must promise to marry her as soon as he returns. Roby firmly promised that he intended to do those very things, and it would be, in fact, very soon.

The newspapers and the rumors all carried the same reports and ideas that the Confederacy was done, that the war would soon be over, and that when General Lee surrendered his troops in Virginia, soldiers would be coming home. Roby was sure that it was time for his father to come home, and rode away with the determination to return to their 1280 acres of old-growth timber with his father. They could then continue cutting and milling lumber for the railroads, and he could finish building a fine cabin for Anna. They could all continue with their lives just as before.

* * *

It was not a difficult task to find that Captain Robert Martin was leading a company of cavalry to meet and slow the advance of Stoneman's raiders through Asheville, Boone, and Wilkesboro in his Carolinas campaign. All Roby had to do was say he had been assigned to Martin's Company and directions followed. Stoneman intended to block Lee's retreat from Virginia, however, the most recent dispatches said that General Lee was currently weighing a decision to surrender in Virginia and put an end to the loss of Union and Confederate life.

Employing guerrilla tactics, Martin's small company would engage Stoneman's split regiment in a series of hit-and-run engagements in the strategic locations of Shallowford, Mocksville, Salisbury, and Morganton. Each time, Martin's company attacked the superior force of Union troops that were occupied with destroying tracks, burning factories, and appropriating supplies from the local farmers and merchants.

Roby, moving alone, followed the trail of casualties from previous skirmishes, and it led to his father's severely battle-depleted company at Howards Gap. Stoneman's raiding party was prepared to again destroy rails, bridges, and depots on the route to Asheville, which led Stoneman, eventually, back into Tennessee.

Howard's Gap was a principal route used by settlers, traders, and native Cherokee as it crossed the French Broad

River south of Asheville. The steep gorge to the river provided a hidden perch from which to ambush Stoneman's raiders, and Captain Martin intended to take full advantage of the opportunity.

The rumor of Lee's surrender was not yet a fact but disheartening nonetheless. Martin's cavalry, however, was still determined to make a formidable reduction of Stoneman's force before it could reach Asheville. Because of Lee's inevitable surrender, most were ready for the war to be over and wondered if there was even a home left where they could return.

Arriving soon after Stoneman's party, Roby caught up with Martin's company as he traversed the dense forest ridge above the gorge at Howard's Gap. On the opposite ridge from where he saw Martin's company lying in wait, he also witnessed Stoneman setting up an overwatch of the railroad, bridge, and depot. There was a squad of snipers prepared to unleash hellfire upon Captain Martin's position. The firefight began with a blast from the brush surrounding the bridge, which burst in a cloud of smoke obscuring the view much like the dense fog that rose over the river these mountain mornings.

This time, a squad of Union sharpshooters opened up from the opposite bank above the cloud of smoke. Roby could only watch. Martin's troops fell as quickly as Stoneman's, and Captain Martin was cut down leading his men. Captain Martin died there on the trail during the brief but intense battle. There was nothing Roby could do to prevent it.

Seeing this ambush unfold before his eyes and finding himself without the ability to get word to his father, Roby was so angered that he violently charged through the brush unseen and fired a single shot from his long rifle, striking a Union Soldier who was poorly concealed from the side of the ridge. Taking the soldier's revolver and repeating rifle, Roby jumped into the firefight to, in turn, take the life of another soldier that did not expect an attack from his left flank. The echoing gunfire in the gorge made it impossible to hear or distinguish the direction of the gunfire around them.

Roby killed or wounded a dozen Union soldiers while they were firing on Martin's position. Upon discovering that the soldier he had just killed was even younger than he, Roby fell to his knees with the piercing pain of the knowledge this was not the way men should be forced to treat each other. Seeing the ambush continue to take its toll, Roby gathered more weapons - another sniper's repeating rifle and angrily rejoined the fight with a determination usually seen only in aged veterans. A superior marksman, Roby began eliminating one Union Soldier after the other from his position on the bank. Only when he began to run low on ammunition, Roby abandoned his post and begin to make his way back along the ridge and across the gorge to where his father had fallen. Roby carried his father's lifeless body back to his horse and guided them both out of the gorge and away from the battle.

Soon, the fighting was over and the Union army had severely decimated Martin's company. The remainder of troops on both sides pulled back, quickly retreating. What was left of Martin's calvary moved back into the mountains. Stoneman's force, who had abandoned their efforts to destroy the rails, retreated instead to rejoin their main force in Asheville.

Roby fashioned a drag behind his horse to carry his father and turned back to the mountains, where he still had promises to keep. Now added to his responsibilities, was burying his father on their treasured property on a hilltop next to his mother in Burke County.

The war, drawing to a close by all accounts, would be over soon. It was certainly over for Roby and his father.

THE COMING STORM

1892

Quickly deteriorating, the ridge road was now putting enormous stress on the wagon, the horses, the Sheriff, and the murderer Roby Martin. Reluctant to say anything at all, Roby still felt the need to explain,

"If you keep driving your team this hard, on this road, in this old wagon, you're going to lose them all."

"Shut your mouth." replied the Sheriff over his shoulder. "We're stoppin' soon enough."

After a brutal mile, the road began to turn away from the river and, in the distance, presented them with a wagon stop in the middle of a small clearing. The moment they turned towards the stop, there was a loud crack when the wagon axle broke, crushing the rear wheel and dumping Roby out onto the trail. The trail was on an embankment overlooking the river, and Roby found himself rolling downwards, crashing into underbrush and rhododendron, toward the river, fully unable to stop himself with his shackled limbs. The rain-swollen waters swallowed him up, bouncing him around like an old log from bank to stone with the weight of his shackles dragging him under. Suddenly, he was torn, soaked, and gasping out of the rapids and onto the riverbank by the Sheriff, who had clearly braved the floodwaters to save him.

Martin looked at the Sheriff, opening his mouth to thank him, but before he could catch a breath, the Sheriff got to his feet, not meeting his eyes, said,

"I don't want to hear a word out of you. I should 'a let you drown."

"It could have been worse, I guess," Martin allowed.

"Yeah," the Sheriff replied. "This is worse. I just saved a murderer."

Having just finished the closest resemblance of a conversation in weeks, Roby studied the face of the Sheriff, wondering why he seemed familiar. At his young age, it was impossible to have met before, but there was something there. Something.

The night was spent at the wagon stop shelter with the horses. A fire the size of a buckboard warmed the pair, dried their clothes, and allowed a measure of rest they had not felt in the three weeks since leaving Kentucky. Roby felt the stare of the Sheriff on him, and although he had the urge to ask for his name, again, he was not inclined to attempt another conversation. Cradling his bruised and swollen cheek, Roby curled up on the ground and hoped that sleep would take him.

On horseback, the pace would increase. It would only be another few days before Roby and the Sheriff would make it back to the Burke County jail, where Roby would finally learn more about his charges.

PORTER'S MILL

1867

*A*rriving early at the mill was normal for Roby Martin. He liked to take the time to select well-milled, choice pieces of lumber to take home for special projects. Today, Roby wanted pieces of trim to complete a special project - a chest that Anna's mother wanted for her quilts.

Mrs. Pruitt described the chest as "Smaller than a steamer chest in size, but substantial to last the years. It should have a squared top with leather straps and ornate trim. It must be as strong as the family that owns it."

"I will make it from mountain oak from the Blue Ridge, with a cedar lining using the finest cuts and matching grains. You won't be disappointed, Mrs. Pruitt." Roby had proudly agreed.

For two weeks, Roby milled the wood, assembled the

chest, and finished the oak with flaxseed oil. The chest was a work of art. Roby planned to take the chest to Mrs. Pruitt the following Sunday.

Roby arrived at the mill early on Monday to fashion the leather straps when he saw Cal Porter there, sitting on a lumber wagon, whittling a stick like he was sitting on a porch.

"Saw your wife again Saturday, Roby. You ain't mad, are ya?" Cal challenged Roby.

"A bit early to be drinkin', ain't it, Cal?" Chuckled Roby. "How's yer head? I see that knot is almost the size of the skillet that made it. Yer' hat don't fit just right neither." Roby was amused to see Cal wearing his hat uncomfortably tipped to one side, clearly framing the massive knot on his forehead and a purple bruise on his brow.

Irritated by the burst of laughter from the dozen mill-hands who were now showing up for work and enjoying the altercation, Cal jumped to his feet in the wagon and kicked at Roby's face. Roby, now standing beside the wagon, dodged Cal's foot as the momentum of the kick caused the load to shift and Cal to lose his balance. Cal fell, and the stacked lumber threw him out of the wagon and on top of Roby, where they both fell to the ground, followed by cut wood planks. Cal was on top of Roby, and a dozen milled two-by-six-inch hardwood boards fell on top of Cal. The millhands stood shocked and silent, briefly frozen by surprise.

Four of the hands rushed to the wagon and started lifting the milled wood off of the pair as Roby pushed Cal away.

Roby jumped to his feet and was ready to take Cal on once and for all when Cal staggered to his feet, looking down at his own knife buried deep into his inner thigh.

Pulling the knife out of his thigh, Cal claimed, "You. You cut me wide open!"

"You cut yourself, Cal," Roby corrected him as he watched the blood gushing from Cal's leg, "Jesus, Cal, you got a' git to Doc Pruitt. You're bleedin' somethin' awful."

Cal fell to the ground in shock.

"You tried to kill me cuz'a' Anna."

"You're bleedin' out, Cal. Get in the wagon and into town."

"You killed me, Roby. I'll never make it. I'm done... I'm done...."

Lester Gragg, the mill foreman who, rushing to break up the fight that was sure to come, stood and witnessed, "Roby, he's dyin', he's a'ready turning white. The Porters will have your ass for this. They'll have you arrested. You best run!"

The millhands helped load Cal on the wagon, but Cal Porter died in a pool of blood there at the mill. He bled to death within minutes, with Roby trying to stop the bleeding.

"You best git gone till it's set right. Go, Roby!" cried Gragg. "Go! You know them; you know what they'll do. Go!"

Roby, helping place Cal on the wagon, had tried to stop the bleeding. After seeing Cal bleed out, seeing his blood-covered hands, and the eyes of the millhands, Roby mounted his horse and turned for home. Considering that the Porters were the most powerful family in three counties, the tension between himself and Cal, knowing he didn't have the resources to fight the Porters, Roby left the mill with the intent of finding a place to wait out the truth. He went home.

When he arrived home, Anna was working in the garden before she went to help her father. Roby, still covered in Cal's blood, told her of the accident and how Cal had died there at Porter's mill naming him as the killer. Concerned by the blood, worried but clearheaded, Anna said:

"Roby, you have to go until this is settled and the truth is out. The Porters will be angry and come after you right away. The Sheriff is their man, and he won't wait to find the truth. You have to go. Go to my uncle, Doctor Stillman, in Knoxville, where we can write you and let you know when you can come back. We will find the hands that will tell the truth."

"How can I leave you?" he asked, holding her against him. She pushed her palms against his chest, holding him away so that she could take in the damage. He had a few scratches on him and was a bit worried, but ultimately the blood was not his, and the longer he stood there wearing it, the closer to the danger he got.

"Because if you leave now, it will only be for a short while. If you leave later, it will be at gunpoint, and it could be forever."

Roby knew she was right. He grabbed provisions, a bedroll, and gear for the ride. Roby looked into Anna's green eyes. "Write me as soon as you can."

She paused and pulled him toward the far side of the

cabin, where their bed lay. They embraced each other, and though it was feverish and tinged with the impending doom of the price upon Roby's head, it was still the assurance of their love for each other. It was the last time they would lay together, although neither of them knew it.

"Roby Martin, I love you! I will be here when you get back. I promise!" Anna called from the porch as Roby tacked his horse.

Roby couldn't bring himself to say the words back because it sounded far too much like goodbye. Simply, "I love you." was all Roby could muster.

With three days of provisions, his horse, and gear, Roby rode West towards Tennessee and the Overmountain Trail.

Behind him, Anna's form disappeared in the distance, still watching.

THE OVERMOUNTAIN TRAIL

1866

The Overmountain Trail was a rough and lightly traveled shortcut thru the Blue Ridge Mountains to key and strategic points of land between Asheville and Black Mountain. It skirted Mt. Mitchell and the highest peaks in North Carolina. Over 300 miles long, it was a path through Virginia, Tennessee, North Carolina, and South Carolina used by the American Revolutionary armies in the 1780s to move troops undetected thru the Carolinas to fight the British. In 1866 it was used more by whiskey peddlers to avoid lawmen and "revenooers." The whiskey business was thriving after the Civil War because it was a generational skill and still very much in demand. Because fields had been ravaged or unattended for years during the war, one had to find a way of life by whatever means possible.

Roby Martin was very familiar with the people, the land,

and the trails to Tennessee and the Carolinas. The profitable business of corn liquor was accepted by the Appalachian people as a necessary post-war means of survival. Successful distillers in the South were often considered businessmen and heroes, while people from the North mostly considered them lawless heathens. The only real problem, as Southerners saw it, was the federals placed post-war taxes on property owners and on the sale of whiskey. Unprecedented, the mountain folk saw no reason to pay a tax on a hand-made product or property that had been in their families for generations. The idea of paying a federal tax on their goods and land was completely unacceptable to many.

Not an easy road by wagon, the Overmountain Trail was passable enough for a rider on horseback. Wild game was plentiful, so few rations were needed if the traveler was resourceful. It was not the first time Roby had been on this trail. Much of this trail was followed bringing his father back from Howard's Gap. The brutal memory was compounded now by the realization that every time he took this road, he was actively avoiding federal troops, federal agents, sheriffs, highwaymen, runaways, and now even immigrants. The trail made famous eighty years before by rebel troops that fought the British loyalists for the independence of a newly declared nation of the United States, now still represented a path to freedom for men being hunted and persecuted by those who sought to engage or enslave them.

The first night was easy enough. The air was cool and arid. It allowed Roby to rest comfortably under the stars.

Provisions, too, were good, though he ate only enough to have energy and not a bite more. Skilled as a hunter though he was, he knew it was not a good idea to take the chance of using a rifle and attract undue attention.

Progress was slower than he had hoped. Whenever other travelers, whether they be alone or in groups, came upon him in the distance, Roby was quick to beckon his horse into the trees, watching carefully from the thick underbrush until they passed. Most people would not recognize him, but the last thing he wanted was his location or destination to be discovered and relayed back to the Burke County Sheriff. Roby figured it was better to be safe than be sorry. He imagined Anna, the unsettled look in her eyes as he rode away, and swore to himself that he would return to her in one piece.

The second night was met with rain, and Roby awoke early in the morning with his teeth chattering and covered in ice crystals formed by the frosting mountain air. That morning was another slow start, as he felt the need to start a small fire in order to still the quaking in his bones.

By the fourth day, the rations had been all but picked apart, and Roby decided it was time to do a little bit of hunting. His rifle felt familiar on his shoulder even after so many days without its use, though the air was seeping hungrily into his muscles, giving him a bit of a tremor. Still, it was like greeting an old friend, and he felt at one with it immediately. It didn't take long for him to take down a pair of rabbits, which he trussed up on his horse for later. The meat would be lean and gamey, but he needed to preserve his horse's energy, so there was no point in taking down anything larger.

That night, the fourth, was the first time Roby felt comfortable eating until he was full. He had no preserving supplies with him, no time to dry the meat in the sun, and so anything he didn't eat would likely go to waste anyway, to be picked apart by vultures, bears, or coyotes long after his departure. The weather was kinder, too, and so he went to sleep warm, with a full stomach. When Roby awoke, next to the sizzling embers of his campfire the next morning, he brushed the dew off of his bedroll with new vigor. There were only a few days left in his journey, and then he would be in Knoxville. He would find Dr. Stillman and, possibly, some answers.

On the trail, In the distance, Roby heard the creaking of a wagon, hoof-prints, and a low chatter of multiple riders. Quickly scaling a small hill up a creek bed, dodging brush to gain cover in the higher ground, Roby dismounted and took shelter behind the dense undergrowth and stand of old-maple timber. As he stood silently, calming his horse with his back to a broad maple, the all-too-familiar click of a single-action revolver broke the silence as a simple "shhhhhhh" was the only spoken command. The cold steel of a barrel against his temple kept him from turning to see his captor.

The wagon and riders slowly passed as they chattered on about their River crossing, the provisions they lost, and what they will need to replenish and cover the "Cod Liver Oil" they had in glass jugs. The trek to Columbia after their stop in Pickens would certainly be easier than what they had just experienced in the mountains, and they knew it. "A few bushels of 'taters n' 'greens would cover the jugs" for the trip and would be plentiful in Pickens. The deep-bed wagon was hiding supplies, but Roby had a good notion of what was being transported.

When the riders were well out of earshot, the pressure of a gun barrel eased off of Roby's cheek, and he cautiously turned to see a cocked and loaded Colt .44 caliber pistol still aimed at his face by his boyhood friend.

"Major!" exclaimed Roby, surprised and relieved.

"Hey, Roby. Of all places to see you. I was 'spectin to see you at your cabin later down the road. What's goin' on, and where's Anna?"

Major Lewis Redmond grew up in the hills of North Carolina like Roby and Amos Ladd - Lewis's best friend. They had begun distilling "Poteen," as Redmond's Irish father had expertly called it. Having organized a distribution network in the countryside, Lewis and Amos had been cooking, buying, selling, and running illegal corn whiskey from Asheville to Knoxville and from Pickens all the way to Columbia. Nearly half of the families within 100 miles of Burke County were scratching out a living in post-war North and South Carolina by either growing corn, distilling corn, or running corn liquor to the three surrounding states. They all knew and were complicit in the sale of illegal whiskey organized by Redmond and Ladd. The true and simple fact was Major Lewis Redmond was the South's closest figure to Robin Hood. Dime novels and the northern papers compared him to Billy the Kid and called him "The Outlaw Major Lewis Redmond."

Roby explained what happened with Cal Porter only a week before, and his decision to wait out the law. Roby asked his trusted friend Lewis to check in on Anna when he could.

"She will be glad to know everything is ok and that I'll be in Knoxville in a few days."

"Roby, I'm goin' to Dark Corners," said Lewis.

"Oh no. Major, why?" Roby couldn't believe his ears.

"I killed Al Duckworth, Roby."

"But Lewis, I don't understand. Why Al?"

Al Duckworth was the Sheriff of Caldwell County.

An old friend of the Redmond, Ladd, Martin, and many other families, Al had never tried to interfere with the illegal moonshine operation. He respected that Lewis and Amos provided a means of support for so many families. He knew Lewis also helped pay taxes on their land to enable them to continue to make a living when so many were forced to move west for land to start over. Al had stopped them before and made them pour out the illegal liquor. Once, Al led a posse off in the wrong direction. But now, there was a substantial price on Lewis's head. The times had changed, and Al Duckworth had a job to do.

"He stopped Amos and me on a liquor run and tried to arrest us both.

Roby, He was gonna take us in n' I couldn't let him. They'd a' put us in prison. The federals are after me now. I got to lay low for a bit."

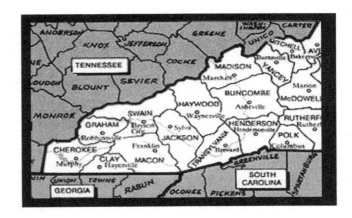

Dark Corners is a legendary camp on the border of Georgia, South Carolina, and North Carolina where no lawman will claim jurisdiction – local or federal. Some claim it was no more than a legend and didn't exist.

But Dark Corners was real. Very real. Outlaws camp there and trust each other for protection. Even the federal marshals refuse to enter the unforgiving mountain territory of laurel hills, sheer cliffs, creek bed trails, and forests so thick it was dark at noon - a rider must dismount and lead his horse in.

A by-product of a brutal war, hundreds of men, camped in the safety of Dark Corners. It would not be the last time Roby would see Lewis or hear about "The Outlaw Major Lewis Redmond."

Those last few days on the trail were only repeats of each other. Roby catching small game, roasting it over a campfire and dodging travelers on the trail. He slowly felt the blow of Cal Porter's final night, Al Duckworth's death, and the loss of his father slough off him with each warm meal and rest. The Smokey Mountains now behind him, he was relieved by the sight of Knoxville across the Tennessee River on the horizon.

KNOXVILLE, TENNESSEE

1867

*A*rriving at the outskirts of Knoxville in the late afternoon, Roby found that the railroad migrant camps in post-war Knoxville offered only a small degree of safety in numbers. There was an immense sort of comfort in anonymity in a sea of strangers, but not these strangers.

The law seldom came into the camps here because if they found who they were looking for, which was unlikely, many migrants would simply not let the deputies take the captive away. The people here were nothing if not loyal, and they were more than willing to fight to no good end to protect one of their own. The camp was not a good resting place, but it would do until Roby could find Dr. Stillman and get word to him that a letter from the Pruitt family was on its way.

Keeping a safe distance by skirting the perimeter of the camp, Roby happened on a family working desperately to repair a broken wheel on their wagon. A small girl, not more than six years of age, tended to a toddler, bouncing him up and down on her lap to keep him entertained. Nearby, her father strained mightily, struggling to lift the wagon bed on his back as high as possible while the mother pushed the wheel back onto the axle where it belonged - almost.

Roby, without hesitation, dismounted and came over to help, joining the father beneath the wagon bed. Together, they were able to lift the wagon high enough for the wheel to slide on somewhat easily.

"Caught me in a tight spot, friend," the wagon owner admitted, "If you'd a been a highwayman, I'd a' been in might' a' trouble."

"Lot's of 'em still out there," admitted Roby. "Plenty a' bad men with no direction right about now."

"War's done that, Sir. Got a name?"

"Roby Martin. And you?"

"Waites Garrett, Mr. Martin, Thanks for the strong back. This here's my wife Claire and my girl Caroline, and that there is my boy little Waites."

Roby tipped his hat, making eye contact with each of the family, "A fine family Mr. Garrett. You're a lucky man. Where ya' headed?"

"We got family out in Wyoming. Too much trouble 'round here, see, too many... what was it you said? Bad men with no direction?"

Roby offered, "Well, I'm a passable Carpenter. I can help you with those wheel spokes if you'll be here a bit longer."

"Much obliged. I'm a blacksmith. I Still gots' some work to do on the axel. The Or'mountain Trail took a toll on this old wagon. She's loaded heavy n' needs some work."

As the travelers thanked Roby profusely for the help, convinced they would not have been able to do it alone, they invited Roby to share their fire, their soup, and their camp for the night. It was clear to see that the Garretts were good people trying to put the war and war's misfortunes behind them. They were post-war immigrants determined to move West, where the country offered more freedom, fewer regulations, and especially fewer regulators.

Waites Garrett was dressed in a white shirt, but his pants were Union blues. Roby considered he had seen enough bad times, too, and was eager to put them behind. They didn't talk of the war or the misfortunes of men - they talked of families, of hope, and the prospect of free government land stakes in the Wyoming territory and the Dakotas.

Roby and Waites spent the next few days strengthening the wagon for the formidable trip that lay ahead. Waites Garrett was a large man, even by blacksmith standards, and able to handle most physical tasks with ease. He followed Roby's instructions without complaint, and Roby, who was not used to having a partner in his work, figured that Waites was the best he had worked alongside. They fashioned the wheel spokes out of black locust wood, which was a dense and stronger wood than oak or fir, and so, much better suited to handle the rigors of the long trip. Roby had been on the trail to Knoxville for too long now, and it was past time to find Dr. Stillman to see if there was any word from Anna.

It was dusk of that day when Roby and Waites were approached by three very desperate-looking men. They didn't approach the camp directly; they took up positions as though they were flanking the camp and sizing it up for an attack. They moved in and started pressing the group for supplies.

"Hey friend, them's your coloreds?" Said the shortest of the three men. addressing Roby.

"Lookin' to me like you got plenty a' food to share." He added.

All three men, haggard and dirty, were unfriendly and suspicious by appearance. Likely hungry, too, Roby knew these men would not take no for an answer. As they mistook Waites and his family for slaves and harmless because of it, the three continued to move in closer on Roby.

"We're just passin' thru, gents. Y'all look healthy enough. We only got what we need; you three best keep movin' along. There's nothin' for ya' here." warned Roby.

Roby moved his hand to one of the discarded oak wheel spokes and used it like a crutch to rise from his seat. The taller man to his left had a deep scar across the eye on the right side of his face. Roby thought that he likely would not see a strike coming from his own right side. As the three men now began to close in and surround Roby and Waites, he gripped the spoke tightly and brought it down with a loud crack, knocking the tallest of the three to the ground. As the tall man floundered, Roby quickly pulled his pistol and set his sight on the third man to his right. The second man, now close in front of him, was tussling with Garrett. One blast by Roby blew the third man off his feet and into the dense underbrush, where he lay motionless with a dime-sized hole where his collar button used to be.

Roby turned quickly to find the shorter, second man bearing down on him with an old flintlock pistol. There was an explosion, and Roby's vision was replaced with blinding white light. Before he had time to react, Garrett was upon the shorter man again, gripping him from behind and snapping his neck as if nothing more than a dry willow branch. Unable to see, Roby turned in the direction of the tall man to his left, who was finally beginning to recover from the wagon spoke that had broken his nose, and aimed his Colt in the direction that Roby last saw him fall. The dazed highwayman raised his arms in surrender.

"No, please, I'm done! I'm done!"

Roby promised him, "You git' now, or you're a dead man. You come back, you won't get this chance again. Git. NOW!"

The tall man ran away from the camp through the brush as if the entire world's devils were on his heels, towards the thickness of the migrant camp. He disappeared, running down the narrow trail into the darkness.

Waites asked Roby, "Are you alright? His gun was in your face. How did he miss?

"Don't feel like he did, answered Roby. I can't see..."

"I don't see no blood cept' this cut on 'ur scalp - gun must a' blowed up. But your face is burnt sumthin' awful. We'll get the wagon packed n' start to move out. You gotta' stick with us, though, till we'll find your doctor. We'll get us a new camp too."

Garrett loaded his family and wagon, tied Roby's horse to the side rail, and moved out quickly as daylight began to break. A new, safer place to camp must be found before the attempt to find a doctor.

The question now was how to find Dr. Stillman?

THE LETTER

1867

*W*aites and Roby, riding together into Knoxville, found the Doctor's Shingle hanging on the main street easily. The many patients ahead of him drew out the wait and as the hour passed, Roby grew more anxious and uneasy.

Being in any town was dangerous for him right now. The lawmen could, at any moment, become aware of his deeds in Burke - not to mention the migrant camp. Only the repeated sentiment that a man with burns like these would go to a doctor's office assured him nothing he was doing was out of the ordinary. It was unlikely he would draw undue attention. Besides, who would recognize him with these burns on his face?

"Next?" the nurse inquired. Waites nodded, and Roby allowed himself to be led to the examination room.

"Powder burns. Hmmm. Not the first time I've seen this." The good Doctor's voice was calm and even, and Roby could hear the soft scratching of pencil against paper.

"Dr. Stillman? I'm Roby Martin, you should have a letter for me."

There was a pause, and a quick deep breath from across the room. "Yes, Mr. Martin, I have a letter. But will you be able to read it?"

"No Sir, not yet, but I plan to." Roby would not allow himself to imagine a world where he could not read this letter.

"I'm going to treat your burns first. It will be some time before you can read, young man. These burns are bad. Your eyes will be bandaged over."

Dr. Stillman reached across his desk to an envelope lying under a Bible and handed it to Roby. It's from Doctor Pruitt in North Carolina – my brother-in-law."

With so much going thru Roby's head, he forgot to thank Dr. Stillman and turned for the door. The nurse took him by the arm and directed him back to the examination table where she would continue to treat and bandage Roby's burns.

The salve the nurse put on his burns gave him remarkable relief from the pain almost instantly. Roby thought, "Sometimes you don't know how much pain you're in until it stops. I suppose that's true of most things."

Roby hoped that the pain of being away from Anna was temporary and that now, clearly, his loss of eyesight was temporary too. For the first time in days, Roby was feeling better. At least until he realized that the letter was from Anna's father.

The letter being from Anna's father took Roby by surprise. Looking forward to hearing from Anna, but, still not yet able to read on his own because of the powder burns, was a difficult mix of anxiety, excitement, and terror. Why had Anna not written herself? Why just the one letter? Why is the letter from her father?

Roby placed the letter in his inside jacket pocket, and left Dr. Stillman's office with Garrett's help. It was time to hurry back to the new riverside camp where they could check on the family and begin healing. The ride back was too quiet as Roby considered the possibilities. He listened for the tell-tale sounds of hoofprints in the underbrush and the cool air which would breathe the arrival of their camp well off the wagon road near the river.

Stepping down from his horse, Roby could sense, but not yet see, the glowing outline of a campfire. He sat on his bedroll next to the glow and wondered how he would read the letter that he was unusually afraid to open. Holding it up in his hands, he could barely sense the outline of the envelope with the campfire behind it, the areas where the shape of it blocked out the light.

It was two days before Roby would lose patience with the pace of healing. Still unable to see, Roby had to ask.

"Waites, can you read this letter to me?"

"Roby, I can't. Never learnt'. Always worked in the fields

or the blacksmith shop. Didn't have a school at home for us, or the time neither. But," Waites added, "Claire can read some."

"Here Roby, hand it to me, I'll try. My mother showed me some ABCs, but ain't had no schoolin.'" Claire attempted to qualify herself.

Claire walked over to Roby and took the letter from his hands. She struggled with Dr. Pruitt's script, "Roby, I can't read this good. They's too many big words I ain't never seen."

"All right, Claire, just read what you can, and trace the big word's letters in the palm of my hand. Can you do that?

"I recon' I can do that, Roby."

As Claire proceeded to sound out the small words and trace the letters of the larger words, Roby began to get an idea of what was happening in his beloved mountains: Federal troops had been moving into the larger cities like Greensboro and Charlotte already, but were not yet in Morganton, Boone, and Lenoir before he was forced to leave. With troops now moving in, they brought hate and disease that was unsettling to all and deadly to some. It was no surprise that it was still unsafe for him to return.

Roby was, however, disturbed to learn of the Smallpox epidemic the troops and federals brought and the loss of life. Then, Claire stumbled over the written words "We lost Anna" and abruptly stopped reading as she held her breath with her hand clasped over her mouth as if she was trying to stop the words from leaving her soul.

Claire, Waites, and Roby were in stunned silence as

Claire started tracing the word hospital in Roby's hand. Roby felt nothing on his hand and would hear nothing else in the letter. The three would not speak the rest of the evening except to hear Claire say,

"I'm sorry Roby, I'm so sorry."

Roby tossed the letter into the fire and sat with his head in his hands. As the burning paper curled into a blue flame, Roby's world had just collapsed. He was crushed. He was broken. He would never have the family that was so important to him Roby was already feeling the pain of being far from home but now felt the emptiness of having no home was overtaking him.

Bent, dazed, and motionless, Roby didn't sleep, didn't move, and didn't speak the entire night. Roby was sure the pain of this would never release it's grip on his heart.

My Dear Boy,

This is an extremely difficult letter to write.

Federal troops are stationed throughout the county to protect the hospital, the factories, and Porter's Mill. The Porter's loyalty to the Union has brought them much favor among the Unionists. They have vowed to enlist the help of the Sheriff's office and federal troops to find and return you to Burke County where they intend to hang you for murder. It is as we expected – you are not safe here. Your innocence is not yet apparent to all.

New Union troops brought an epidemic of Smallpox into the population of Burke County. All of our families have been affected and hundreds have died before they could be found and treated. We endeavored to reach all those affected, but they were too widespread and many. We lost Anna to the hospital in Morganton where she helped with treatment and will continue her medical studies. Without her help here, we couldn't care for all the families in Edgemont and the Globe communities. Many of your friends were lost.

This is not a good time to think of coming home. Fortune is not yet in your favor. We have not however, given up. I will write again soon to keep you informed. You are missed. Mrs. Pruitt sends her love as always.

Respectfully,

James Pruitt, MD

KENTUCKY

1867

*L*ess than a week after the news, Roby and the Garretts packed up their belongings and continued the move west. His eyesight was slowly beginning to return, and Roby was glad for it. There was more he could do now, at least as a navigator. Their first stop would be on the outskirts of Nashville as marked on their map in a dusty charcoal circle. Pointing further North thru Kentucky and into Ohio, they would pick up the trail West to Wyoming.

Two years before, the battle of Nashville had left the rail-yards and city in a condition much like Knoxville. Post-war migrant camps, highwaymen, and regulators ruled the city and surrounding countryside, making the trail much more dangerous. After a rather stressful journey avoiding Nashville camps by skirting roads to the north, the small party finally reached a town named Beaver Dam. They set up a camp, and for the next short while, Roby and Waites made the banks of the Green River their temporary home.

As though the war had passed them by, Beaver Dam was a quiet and peaceful town. One could even call the pleasant attitudes of its residents a little naive. The townspeople would prove to be some of the finest people Roby had ever met.

It was three weeks before Roby would go into town alone. Knowing the party would be moving out soon, spirits continued to be low, and he was looking to cheer Caroline, little Waites, and himself up with a gift of some sort. Figuring he would pay a quick visit to a general mercantile, he saddled his horse and rode into town alone.

Roby hadn't gotten very far before he found himself in front of a stunning building. The ornate script on the sign presented it as the Beaver Dam Church of God. Drawn to the delicate craftsmanship, Roby found himself dismounting to get a long satisfying look. There was comfort in its lines and design, and Roby was lightly touched with peace for the first time in months.

Across the road stood what appeared to be the humble beginnings of a schoolhouse. Right then, it was just a roof and four walls - nothing close to the thought and care that had been put into the church. Obviously, the structure was not borne of the same builder. He glanced back and forth between the two buildings, comparing their make, until his rather suspicious actions drew the attention of a woman inside the school.

"May I help you, mister?" she asked, walking out of the building with a determined stride. Her eyes locked onto Roby's as she moved closer. Her stance, he thought, was guarded, like she might be suspicious of his intentions.

"Uhh, No ma'am, jus' lookin' at the church. Fine handiwork, truly."

"And my school?"

Roby, who hadn't expected to be interrogated, stepped back in surprise. "Ah. Yes, ma'am. The school. Your school?"

"Well, I teach here, so I'd rather hope I can call it mine. Were you looking for something?"

"No ma'am. Looks like you could use a carpenter though." Roby said somewhat awkwardly.

It took an element of self-control for Roby to stop from slapping his hand over his mouth. He had no idea where such a jab had come from. Perhaps from his father? The schoolteacher tilted her head, eyeing him up and down.

"He was killed in the war. Are you some sort of a carpenter?"

Roby had come into town looking for a trinket from a general store, not for a confrontation. He figured it would be best to back down a might.

"I'm sorry, ma'am, I wasn't tryin' to..."

"You didn't answer my question, mister."

"I, yes, ma'am, I'm a carpenter."

"And your name, carpenter?"

"Roby, ma'am, Roby Martin."

The schoolteacher gave him a half-smile, relaxing her posture a little. It was obvious now that he was no threat.

"I am Mrs. Prentiss," the intuitive woman said.

Roby nodded, grateful that the awkwardness had ended amicably. He wasn't particularly used to speaking with women somewhat his senior in such friendly terms.

The schoolteacher took another step closer to Roby looking him in the eyes and asked, "Are you good?"

Roby touched the scars on his face and around his eyes. "Oh, yes ma'am. I'm healing. It's getting better every day and doesn't hurt that much any more. I can at least see now."

Now holding back a proper smile, Mrs. Prentiss said, "Mr. Martin, are you a good carpenter?"

"Oh. Oh, yes ma'am, I'm very good but..."

"It's settled, then! You can start on Monday. You'll give this schoolhouse the attention it deserves."

With that, Sarah Prentiss turned and began to walk back into the schoolhouse, leaving Roby stunned in the street.

In the moment, Roby added, "There's just one thing ma'am..."

* * *

ROBY RETURNED to camp just before dusk, still utterly astonished by the day's events. The image of the school-teacher settled in his head like a blanket against the cold. It made grooming his horse take longer than usual. As they sat around the fire that night, eating their meal, Waites turned to him, saying, "Roby, the horses are healthy, and the party is strong again. I think it's time we get outta here, don't ya' think?"

Roby paused and shook his head. "Waites, I won't be goin' with y'all. I need to stop runnin'. I've been offered work up in the town, and I gotta take it."

"Well," Waites said, nodding, "I can't say I ain't sorry. Yer' a good man, and you're good to travel with. We'll always have a spot for ya' if ya' change yer' mind."

"Thanks for helpin' me when I was blinded, Waites. I've got something for ya'." Roby dug around in his pack, pulling out a school reader.

"It's a primer from the schoolhouse. Claire can use it - teach the young 'uns to read, give 'em some advantage out there."

THE SCHOOLHOUSE

1868

*R*oby arrived at the schoolhouse early in the morning. He inspected the structure and found a solid foundation with few amenities. The door was tight, but a simple bar lock and leather hinges needed to be replaced. The windows were solid to keep out the cold but not louvered to allow air in the summer. A threshing floor was a sign of scarce funding and a hurried build – all things that would be remedied by Roby in the coming years.

* * *

"Mr. Martin, I brought lunch. Will you join me?" Mrs. Prentiss extended a long-overdue invitation to Roby.

Wild Game was getting harder to find along the Green

River, so Roby had moved camp several times since arriving. A homemade meal sounded good since campfire fish was his staple these days. Roby accepted the invitation graciously while hiding the warm feeling it gave him to be sharing a meal with Mrs. Prentiss.

Taking a seat at the study table he had built for the students years before, Roby felt a bit uncomfortable when he realized the chair was so small for him. Crafted for a child, it was quite narrow in the seat for a grown man. Covering her smile with her left hand, Sarah Prentiss reached for her desk chair and pulled it over.

"I'm fine, Ma'am," Roby attempted to intercede.

"Nonsense, you are uncomfortable." The teacher said, still holding back a laugh.

"I invited you today because we need to discuss your future here."

"Ma'am?" Having had the same concern for quite a while, Roby was relieved that this would not be a difficult subject to discuss. However, dead silence promptly filled the schoolhouse for the longest time.

"Roby, have you seen the storage building behind the church?" Mrs. Prentiss broke the silence after a long and very awkward few minutes.

"I have," He admitted. "Reverend Perch asked me if the wood there was good enough for a new pulpit. Most of it is cedar or pine, but there's enough oak left for a very nice, a proper pulpit."

"The reverend told me he would be happy to let you live in the building if you want to stay. There is so much work still to do."

"He did make me that offer." admitted Roby, "I told him I would think it over."

"Roby, we want you to stay. I want you to stay. I want you to call me Sarah, and I want to bring you lunch."

This came as a surprise to Roby even though he had similar feelings. He was comfortable with the arrangements but not with the camping. Roby had been unable to decide on a piece of property. The idea of such commitment to property stirred the pain of his past. Roby had lost so much; and many people in his life that it still weighed on him heavily.

The work kept him busy and focused, the town was friendly, and Roby found Sarah very easy to be around. Though she was a bit older, she was attractive and pleasant company. Although a bit thin, almost frail, she presented herself as strong and was regarded as nothing less. Sarah was fun to talk with, and it seemed she was always building a smile when Roby spoke about his past.

Roby had just read a Hartford, Ky newspaper that put him deep in thought. On the front page, the short article announced that the Murderous Outlaw Major Lewis Redmond was believed to be killed along with his partner Amos Ladd in a shootout at his home in South Carolina. Seeing the concern in Sarah's eyes, Roby tried to put her at ease by telling her how Lewis got the title of "Major" many years ago.

"Lewis was working in a cornfield one day as a boy and heard a soulful sound coming from outside the cornfield not far away. Mesmerized, he went to investigate what was surely Gabriel's horn, only to find a Confederate encampment playing Taps, announcing that the troops would be retiring for the day.

In the following days, the company's Captain would see Lewis observing the training and invited him over for a treat of ginger tea. For weeks, Lewis ran errands, fetched, marched, and trained for the troop's Captain. Lewis became fascinated with his new family. One day, in a solemn ceremony, the Confederate Army Captain bestowed on Lewis, "For conspicuous dedication in the performance of his duties, the honorary title of "Major." He was then officially "Major" Lewis Redmond in title, even if not in rank.

Now, after this article in Kentucky, he is known as "The Murderous Outlaw Major Lewis Redmond." However, in the Carolinas, Lewis was a hero that employed families and paid unjust taxes for struggling landowners."

Roby was saddened by the article written like a penny dreadful, but Roby knew Lewis. He knew better.

Sarah was learning everything about Roby and was comfortable knowing this good man and that he was worthy of her trust. For Roby, it was comforting that Sarah's green eyes reminded him of Anna and how she counted on him for strength. It made him feel at home at times.

"I would like to stay," admitted Roby. "I will speak to Reverend Perch again and renovate the building after I build his pulpit."

"Oh, and Sarah, I want you to know something - I'm sick of fish," Roby smiled.

EDUCATION

1874

*E*ducation was important to Roby. He often thought about Anna's desire to continue her studies with her father and his own inability to continue his studies after the war. He was concerned with the Garrett family's failure to read well and impressed with Sarah's eagerness to gift a reading primer to a family she had never met.

Within 10 years, with Sarah's guidance, Roby advanced his own education and skills to include structural design, building, and road construction. Roby had become a school board member and was appointed commissioner of roads. Roby was beginning to become very popular and influential in Ohio County as well as an important part of Sarah's life.

Roby and Sarah would accompany each other to events, work, meetings, and Church. As widowers, townspeople thought nothing of their time together and accepted that they were destined to be a couple. Neither Roby nor Sarah was concerned with or prepared to take their close relationship to another level.

It was when Sarah fell ill in the winter of 1880 that the inevitable question was raised by the Reverend Perch:

"So, when are y'all gonna' talk about it?"

"Talk about what, Sam?" Roby needed clarification.

"Gettin' married, a' course. You can't stay here takin' care of Sarah without bein' married. Awww, heck, you might as well be married. Ya' spend all your time together. if I'd a' ever seen you two fight, I'd swear you were already married."

The Ohio County Doctor, their friend, Thom Wills, had instructed Sarah earlier in the day to stay in bed for a week and fight the chest congestion with hot soups, quinine, and rest. Ordered to stop working so hard and get some rest, Sarah understood she was to stay in bed and be nursed back to health. Pleurisy was a grave concern.

Roby's eyes turned to Sarah, who was, as usual, holding back a smile.

"Well, right now, if you like, Sarah." Roby finally smiled.

Roby and Sarah married ten days later in the Church where they had met. The entire town of Beaver Dam and many from Hartford attended. Weak, but able to walk with grace, Sarah stood tall and proud to marry Roby, whom she had admired for many years. She married the man who helped her heal from the broken heart of losing her husband in the war between the states.

POLITICS

1892

*R*oby would never forget how much his father had despised politics, politicians, and the lawyers that crafted unjust laws that strangled the mountain families. But, being appointed to the County Commission as Commissioner of Roads and Buildings and elected to the School Board softened the idea a bit for Roby. Then, negotiating with state representatives from Louisville and Evansville opened his eyes to the possibility of the greater good that could be done for others.

What remained unchanged, however, was that Roby, constantly wary of politicians, expected the worst. Hence, he typically found the best in people as they proved their character with actions not intent. Forced to work with lawyers, Roby began to understand that they had a job to do and that they were not every single one like Jacob Small. Blessed with common sense, a will to serve people, a pleasant face, and a likable demeanor, Roby became more popular than he ever cared to be. It was not an easy transition for Roby and certainly not one that he intended for personal gain.

Roby's political aspirations stopped immediately however, when he was summoned to Hartford and approached by John D. Harris of Louisville to run for an upcoming senate seat. The idea of leaving Beaver Dam was now unthinkable. It was an immediate and emphatic "No." Leaving Sarah, who did not travel well, was not an option, and there was still too much work to finish. The school planned to expand to five classrooms, and the Town Hall was slowly transitioning into a community center.

Not one to take no for an answer, and despite Roby's lack of desire to advance in political office, John D. Harris, the at-Large Delegate at the 1890 National convention, announced Roby Martin as a promising, up-and-coming talent with a strong future in Kentucky politics. He described Roby's achievements with enough enthusiasm that he was able to draw everyone's attention. In an election year, this made headlines in Kentucky and Ohio. The notion would travel from Louisville to Hartford and on to Washington. Eventually, the headlines spread to the Carolinas where, one day, Bill Padgett came across the report in a Raleigh Newspaper. The word of Roby Martin's life and whereabouts had just arrived in Burke County, and it was the local newspaperman's duty to report it.

It was a brutally cold winter morning when the publisher

of the Burke County Gazette walked into Sheriff Robert Martin's office. With the next day's paper in his hand, he sat quietly in front of Sheriff Martin's desk.

Sheriff Martin had never seen Bill Padgett speechless before.

"WHAT?"

Padgett had no idea what this information would do to Sheriff Martin.

Understanding fully that the news of his father's good health and location would be a shock, he hoped that Martin would be happy to hear that his father was alive and well. Padgett feared the worst, however. He knew the Martin family's history with politics and government. Still, the publisher was unsure how the Sheriff would react to the news of his father's standing in the political community. One thing he was sure of; Roby Martin's marital status would not sit well with anyone.

"You'll want to see this before everybody in Burke sees it in tomorrow's paper, Robert."

Paggett handed the paper to the Sheriff. It was already folded to the smaller front-page article that announced his father's location and high status in the Kentucky Political community. It went on to detail Roby's marital status and presumed good health.

Leaning back in a momentary freeze, Sheriff Martin stared at the article as if he was still reading for an uncomfortable time. Finally, he rose from his chair, thanked the publisher, grabbed his hat and coat, and declared, "I'm going to get him."

Robert went to his mother first and shared the news article. He explained what little he knew as Anna sat stunned and silent and fighting tears. She finally exhaled in relief as her son assured her, "I'm bringing him back. We're going to have answers..."

Robert packed his wagon with supplies and cinched his horses to leave in the pre-dawn light. First securing a federal warrant, he headed West to bring the fugitive Roby Martin back to North Carolina. He will stand trial for the murder of Cal Porter twenty-five years ago and a second charge which stuck in the Sheriff's craw - adultery.

THE ARREST

1892

$\mathcal{T}$he Ohio County seat was in Hartford, Ky. Only two miles from Beaver Dam. Roby had helped to rebuild it many years after it was burned to the ground by Confederate troops. The Hartford College now existed in the Ohio County School Board administrative offices.

Roby spent less of his time there in the office because of Sarah's declining health, but today, at the courthouse, Roby would address the School Board Commission. He had a plan regarding the expansion of Hartford College in the same building.

The Ohio County Sheriff entered the chambers in the early afternoon of 1892 with the Burke County Sheriff beside him. Roby Martin was addressing the county commission. As Sheriff Wills loudly called on the Mayor of Hartford and the School Board to allow him to interrupt the proceedings, the Burke County Sheriff did not wait for permission and stepped forward grabbing Roby's arm, and announced loudly, "Roby Martin, you are under arrest for the murder of Cal Porter in Burke County, North Carolina in 1867."

"Now hold on there!" Blurted the Chairman of the School Board leaping out of his chair.

"He has a federal warrant, Jack, It's legal. There's nothin' we can do." Sheriff Wills instructed the Chairman, Jack Farmer, watching from only a few feet away as Roby was manhandled and pulled away from a podium he had built with his own hands.

Sheriff Martin checked Roby for a weapon while pulling him towards, and forcefully out of, the large double door that exited the council gallery.

The Burke County Sheriff shackled Roby and tied him in the back of his buckboard. He immediately propped his Rifle up as if to warn those now filing out of the doors and into the street, that he was ready for trouble and would put up with none. Sheriff Martin did not hesitate to leave nor did he answer any of the questions now being shouted from the crowd still filing out of the council doors. He quickly turned his team South towards Nashville meaning to return to Burke County – over two hundred miles away. It was going to be a longer trip than either of them would imagine.

"Guess I knew this might happen someday." Roby spoke to the Sheriff. "Murder, huh? But after twenty-five years?"

"Oh, it's worse than that old man, now shut up. We got a

long ride ahead and I don't want to hear a word you got to say till' your trial."

THE CHARGES

*R*oby Martin was put into a secure jail cell in the Burke County Jailhouse.

The Sheriff said simply, "I'll see to it your Lawyer is here in the morning." With that, the doors were locked, and Roby was alone.

The Jailhouse was much larger than he remembered it twenty-five years ago when Roby crafted the secure door for the old single-cell jail. It was now five empty cells except for Roby Martin.

A bench-like bed, a blanket, a bucket, a desk, and a chair were the surprisingly ample amenities available to him as the prisoner. Roby thought, "Not the comforts of home, but at least I don't have to sit and sleep in the bed of a wagon or on the floor."

Expecting another sleepless night and unable to find any

more information about the trial, Roby leaned back on the plank bed with a wool bedroll under his head. There was no horse's gait, bouncing saddle, rocking wagon, driving rain, creaking axel, or night chill to distract him from the warmth and relative comfort of the cell. His cell shared the heat of a well-tended fire in the Sheriff's office. Roby fell into a deep sleep for the first time since he left Kentucky.

* * *

STARTLED AWAKE by the loud clang of an iron cell door, Roby rose to see the Sheriff opening the barred door. There was a stranger identified only as "Your only friend around here" by the familiar Sheriff.

"Your wife has retained me to argue in your defense. Mr. Martin." announced the unfamiliar middle-aged man with a leather-bound stack of papers and a serious, determined disposition.

"Sheriff Martin was right. You have few friends here, Sir. This will not be easy. Let's go over the charges."

"Sir, did you say Sheriff Martin?" Roby was still shaking off his sleep when what he heard confused him.

"That won't work in your favor, Mr. Martin. He doesn't understand why you never came back. The adultery charge is what you have to fight. Nobody cares about a murder from twenty-five years ago, but everybody wants to know where you've been."

"Adultery?"

"Yes, Anna retained me to represent you, Mr. Martin. Some are surprised, but she wants you to have a Lawyer."

Roby slowly fell back against the wall in shock. He was unable to comprehend that not only was Anna alive, but he also had a son who was now the Burke County Sheriff. Roby's Son was the driven Sheriff that made the unimaginable trip to Kentucky to arrest him at the Courthouse? The same Sheriff that brought him back tied in the back of an open wagon is his twenty-five-year-old Son?

Nothing made sense now.

"Mr. Martin?" asked the Lawyer, "Are you still with me?"

"Sir, we have to go over these charges." He continued. "I am Joseph Pearce."

Roby's attorney introduced himself, but the revelations pouring from him were a flood of confusion that left Roby unable to process them all at once.

"Anna is alive?"

"Yes, Mr. Martin. She asked me to be your Lawyer."

"She, we, have a son?"

"Yes, Sir. Robert is the Sheriff that brought you in. Is this all news to you, Mr. Martin?"

"I received a letter that Anna was lost to smallpox."

"No, Sir. She is the Doctor at the hospital, and until a month ago, everyone but she thought you might be dead."

"Those are nasty scars on your face. You have seen some trouble yourself." Roby's defense attorney observed.

"I don't suppose Cal Porter is alive."

"Quite dead, Sir. Died that day at the mill almost twenty-five years ago. Mr. Martin, would you like to tell me what happened?"

For most of the day, Roby and his Lawyer detailed and scribed that day at Porter's mill, the events in Knoxville, and how Roby settled in Kentucky. It was clear that Roby had intended to return to Burke until he thought there was no reason to ever return.

"It's quite a story, Mr. Martin. My job is to make the jury believe it. Running is not in your favor, Sir, and there are few witnesses left that can corroborate your description of the events that morning at Porter's Mill."

"Anna will be by your side, but we must get through a determined and focused prosecutor. He will not go lightly. You must be careful what you say – he will trap you."

THE TRIAL

The rows of chairs in the courtroom were full for the trial. Usually, the streets around this time of day would be nearly empty. Still, the excitement seemed to have pulled every tottering old woman off her stoop and every grim-faced barkeep away from his whiskey. There was an electric atmosphere to the crowd, which seemed to shadow the Thomas Dula murder trial in Statesville. Dula had been found guilty of killing his girlfriend, Laura Foster, twenty years earlier. The crowds drawn from that trial only barely rivaled this one.

In 1867, a killing under such questionable circumstances would have likely been dismissed as accidental if it were not for the apparent influence of the Porter family. In this case, however, a charge of adultery demanded the attention of the entire South. Unlike any other case, a man having two wives was a moral issue. The reporters, dignitaries, carnival vendors, and the curious would make this unlike any other trial of the era.

Inside the courthouse, it was as though the sun had stopped at the door. The streets were filled with energy, but the walls seemed almost stifling, every whisper echoing ominously through the room. Jack Farmer, the owner of the Hartford General Store, had just arrived determined to relay the goings-on of the courthouse to Sarah Martin.

Sarah, who was unable to travel 200 miles, sent Jack Farmer, who was authorized to secure a defense attorney. Sarah sent her unquestionable love because she already knew the details of what had happened. Her only concern was, like most, the jury mistaking the morality charge and the moral man. Also, Sarah sent the promise to mortgage their house to pay for Roby's defense. Roby would have the representation she believed he deserved at any cost.

In truth, the community was reasonably sympathetic to Roby's predicament and had been the entire time. There were many elements to the case, but the romantic ones, in particular, seemed to draw a bit more pity than anyone had expected. Add to that how much time had passed since the initial crime; it was like the perfect brew for sympathy. Two of the lawyers on the case had been children at the time of the murder, most of the witnesses had long since died or moved west, and memories were growing foggy. Twenty-five years could do a lot to the integrity of a case.

Anna had come down to the courthouse to see Roby and

to take her place beside him, offering all her support with a gentle hand on his arm. Sarah had sent Jack in her stead, but still, it was apparent to all the onlookers that both women very much loved him. And, if his hand on Anna's waist and the whispers he sent Jack's way were evidence, Roby loved both of them just as much. One woman had grown with him and shared his youth, the other had been happy to have him in his middle age, and he seemed to have his heart equally divided among them. It was no surprise, then, that Roby Martin's wives were much more attractive to the public than a twenty-five-year-old murder case with no hard evidence.

Folding chairs for the witnesses are placed in neat rows on the courtroom floor and are quickly filled with spectators. Women are allowed to stay for Anna, though usually, they would be turned away at the door. Judge A.C. Avery enters through the door beside the rostrum, hangs up his hat, and seats himself, adjusting his wire-rim glasses as he takes in the crowd.

The clerk of court makes his way down the center aisle to pull the bell rope hanging from the ceiling and announces:

"All those wanting justice in the State of North Carolina will draw nigh to the bar."

The solicitor, Benjamin Miller, a private prosecution counsel, and the two defense attorneys take their places. Roby is led in; A tall, grey man, in his suit, in his hair, even in his complexion; like the cell had worn the color out of him. Anna Martin sits beside him, her auburn hair pulled back into a tightly-woven bun. A grey streak makes its way through the red, coiling like a snake around a green ribbon. Her eyes are just as green as Roby remembers, and it is clear to everyone in the room that he can't tear his eyes away. Anna smiles at him, and the smile is forgiveness. She knows that he is an innocent man.

The trial begins with witnesses. Jonah Shuman is first, Cal Porter's uncle by marriage and an eyewitness to the crime.

"I remember Cal, uh, M r . Porter, I mean, was sittin' on the roller bed with a group of men waiting on the mill. Martin came up, and I heard Porter say to the others, he says, 'fel-las, don't let him kill me!'"

The crowd rumbles, and the Judge holds up a steady hand, motioning for Shuman to continue:

"Mart Taylor, God rest his soul, pulled them apart, but not fast enough, I suppose. Martin had - well, he'd cut three deep gashes in Porter's leg. Severed an artery, see, and he bled out. Jus' like that."

Next is Mary Porter, Cal Porter's daughter.
"My father was a... liked to drink, that is," she admits, fiddling uncomfortably with the lace on her sleeves. "He often did it, and I know he had a bit the day of the murder, but I do not believe he was drunk right then. He went over to the cabin, the Martin cabin, that is, to borrow some tobacco."

"Martin said no. And father... he was tellin' one of the boys about it later, and I overheard. He said he had threatened Martin's job and would turn 'im out. And Martin said that... if he did, he'd kill him."

The silence was broken as someone in the back of the crowd gasped, and Anna clutched Roby's sleeve, pulling him close. It took him back to the days when Anna would run her hand up his sleeve and stretch it out. It made him wish he wasn't in a suit.

"I was up by the roller when it happened. I saw Martin slash at father twice, and after he had gone, father said, 'bury me on the hillside, boys. Roby Martin has killed me.'"

Subsequent testimony and questioning by Roby's young lawyer discloses that Porter had not been to the Martin cabin the morning of the death. It was also established that Roby did not chew tobacco and that Mary Porter, who denied hearing the loud argument preceding the cutting, could hardly have heard her father's last words at so great a distance - if, in fact, it was ever established that he spoke them.

The State's last witness, Ruth Ware, a fourteen-year-old girl at the time of the murder, who had come down to the mill to see her sweetheart, swears that she saw Roby grab Cal's leg and cut three licks in it with his knife. Except for the number of gashes, she substantiates the daughter's story.

Then, the State rests. So far, the testimony has run smoothly. The solicitor has dealt gently with his witnesses, and the defense attorneys have been courteous in cross-examination.

Next, Roby is called to speak in his own defense. He

recounts the morning of the crime as being a bit early to see Cal with a "snoot full." The crowd roars, with Judge Avery slamming his gavel to silence them.

"This is no laughing matter," he says before leveling his gaze at Roby. "I expect decorum in my courthouse!"

Roby throws up his hands. "Yes, Sir, I meant to say I had no intention of fighting a drunk man. The drunkenness is what must have made him fall. He knocked over the lumber that way; it fell on us both."

For the first time, the event has been described as an accident and possibly an unintentional act resulting in the death of Cal Porter. Long since dead, Lester Gragg, the Mill Foreman, is no longer there to support the accident or the importance that Roby should run until the truth be told.

The story's thread has been continually broken by objections from the prosecution and spirited tilts between the opposing attorneys for the admission of telling bits of evidence. Everyone leans forward to listen, and Judge Avery stops the proceedings to give the ladies time to leave the courtroom. Roby was instructed to tell the court precisely what Anna told him about that morning on the porch of his cabin between Anna and Cal.

Judge Avery, expecting sensitive testimony, instructs the women to leave the courtroom. They do sort themselves out of the courtroom, however reluctantly. The Deputy herds them into a room beside the Judge's rostrum full of maintenance equipment, old ballot boxes, and odds and ends from old political campaigns – everything but chairs. Though the

Deputy thoughtfully leaves the door slightly ajar, Sheriff Martin comes by and closes it tightly.

The hum of voices in the courtroom goes on and on. After a long time, chairs begin to scrape across the courtroom floor. Inside the storage room, there is general confusion about what is happening. One of the women looks out to find the court is leaving for dinner, having forgotten the women are closed in their room. In the meantime, they have missed all the testimony about the years Roby Martin had spent in Kentucky, which followed the brief scandalous bit of testimony they were not allowed to hear. The ladies filed out of the storage room extremely unhappy.

The Solicitor, Benjamin Miller, begins his cross-examination after the lunch break ragging, contradicting, interrupting, and restarting with confusing conclusions. Roby looks withdrawn and unhappy, but his answers are thoughtful, unhurried, and courteous. The solicitor demands to see exactly how the murder was committed. To do so, he climbs upon the lawyers' table as if it were a lumber wagon and asks the prisoner to put him in precisely the same position that Porter had been in the wagon. While attempting to confuse Roby as much as possible, Miller continued with the repeated question, "You say it was like this. Are you sure? Put me in the exact position Porter was!"

"That is as near as I can make it," says Roby, his voice tinted with defeat.

"I said just exactly, not something like it," demands the solicitor and so on, for ten minutes until he realizes that Roby has just stood him up on the desk, standing on one leg, with his left hand pointing in the air, and the right hand covering his groin. The solicitor's face turns red as the courtroom bursts into laughter. Miller jumps back onto the floor with furrowed eyebrows, eyeing the crowd as though daring them to continue laughing. Holding back a laugh himself, Judge Avery, who had since grown restless with the solicitor's harassment of the defendant, reminded Roby that he did not want the proceedings to become a spectacle and that he would do well to testify honestly and directly on his own behalf.

The solicitor continues, "Now take this knife and show me how you did it."

"I never had his knife. I got one of my own." replied Roby, "Cal cut himself when he fell on it."

The solicitor tries to trap Roby into admitting he had cut Cal - without success. Finally, a new witness was called. This witness was for the defense.

A trembling older man in neat black clothes, his back bent over so that he can only peer upward, approaches the witness stand. His face was yellow with wasting disease, and he had been sitting among the witnesses. He attracted little attention until he was called to testify. He turns out to be the coroner who had examined Cal Porter as he lay in the mortuary so many years ago, now living in Greensboro.

"I found," he says, voice wavering, "one cut, two inches long and one and a-half-inch deep, in his thigh. He would've limped off normally, but somehow the knife had sliced his artery completely. An accident, I said, even back then. It never looked like anything else."

If the audience thought the cross-examination of the older man would be civil out of consideration of his frailty, they would be disappointed. The prosecutor harries him endlessly, breaking in on the weak old voice, pointing out his deformity, and dragging out an admission that he takes dope. Then the solicitor pounces on the coroner and forces him to answer the question,

"Tell this court why you take dope!"

The simple answer quiets any further questions on the

subject, "The morphine is for my back. The disease that bows it causes terrible pain, and it was the only thing prescribed to me that works."

The spirit in the courtroom is now changing, growing quieter and distinctly angry. The cross-examination resembles whipping a horse tied up short in a stall.

Then, the last witness for the defense is called. A surprise witness - a kind older man with horn-rimmed spectacles that proves to have been at the mill that morning to ask for a job. Charles Warren of Mountain City, Tennessee, testifies that he saw Porter whittling a stick with a small penknife in his hand:

"Porter kicked at Martin. I saw the load under his feet shift, and then the entire load, the wood, and Cal Porter were dumped on the ground. They got Martin up, and he posed for a fight, but when they pulled the wood off of Porter, he got up with a knot on his head and his own knife buried in his thigh, cursing the heavens and promising to make Martin pay. He got up and then fell right back down kinda' wild-eyed."

The testimony falls like a bombshell on the court proceedings. It clearly pleased the jury as they nodded their heads in agreement looking at one another. The solicitor was surprised and at a loss for words. He let it pass, intending to gain some ground in cross-examination. The audience wants to clap, but Judge Avery's stern look only allows whispers and shuffles.

The prosecution sets out to discredit his testimony, not

by mentioning that he is illiterate, but by using his ignorance of figures to cast doubt on his intelligence. The solicitor tries to trap him with question after question that would puzzle anyone under the strain of being on the witness stand, even if he knew his arithmetic.

"How old were you in 1867? Oh, but you told me you were 14 when you came to North Carolina in 1865? Don't you know how old you are? Don't you tell the truth? What's wrong with your eyes? What do you wear those glasses for? Can't you see?

The witness answers that he has had to wear them since he was kicked in the face by a mule some time ago.

"And you haven't been very bright since? Can't you tell the truth since the Mule kicked you? Don't the neighbors say you can't tell the truth?"

After more baiting with the numbers, the Defense attorney stops it with one last question.

"Mr. Warren, How much schooling have you had?"

The man adjusts his glasses, looking sheepishly down at the floor. "None at all, sir. There was no opportunity for it when I was growin'."

Most jurors are farmers who know how hard it was to get schooling twenty or thirty years ago in the hills. Plenty of people in the audience can read little or none, not because they did not want to learn. They put themselves in the witness's place. The patience of the entire room is now on a short tether. The solicitor is hurting his case. Understanding the frail barrier between thought and action in the hills, one can only marvel that there have not yet been angry words or actions exchanged by either witness or audience. But, one dark-browed man from Wilson's Creek, called subsequentially as a character witness, stares at the solicitor with a scowl so belligerent that he is treated with careful respect - possibly sensing the whisper running along the aisles:

"He better go easy on that one, or he'll find himself pickin' up teeth for it."

The court finally adjourns for the night after depositions from Kentucky and Wyoming establishing the excellent character of the accused are read into the record. Ten witnesses have testified to Roby's good moral character and Cal's lack of one - how he was often dangerous and quarrelsome with liquor. The solicitor shakes off his robes of violence and becomes the affable man he appears. He has pushed the State's case to the utmost and never once tangled himself in the traps he set for the witness. He knows that the State and the audience expect a dramatic prosecution, and he gives it to them. The courtroom clears, and the streets, the hotel porches, café's and saloons begin to fill.

The prosecution and defense summarize their case most of the next day. In the mid-afternoon, Judge Avery delivers his charge and turns the case over to the jury. They file back precisely one hour and ten minutes later with a verdict of Not Guilty.

Pandemonium breaks loose now that the tension is relaxed. The audience claps and stamps. Everyone congratulates everyone else. Anna Martin thanks each juror with tears running down her face. Only Roby sits numb and unmoved without any change of expression. He rises at last to thank the defense attorney and the jurors. Silently, he shakes the hand of each one.

Outside, in the street, everyone wants to congratulate him all at one time, slap his back, and welcome him home as a free man. Roby and Anna are escorted by the Sheriff to the Glen Alpin Café in triumph for their first meal together in over twenty-five years. More questions hang over them, but for now, freedom is enough.

THE MEETING

*A*fter the excitement of the not-guilty verdict was over, in the privacy of the Café, Roby and Anna had the opportunity to talk about what would happen next. Anna knew, through testimony, why Roby couldn't read the letter, why there was confusion, and why he continued to move on. She knew that In 1867 Roby didn't care about the trouble he left behind, only that he had no reason to return since Anna would not be there. If there was a reason to return, it was to visit his mother and father's hilltop graves buried next to each other. Maybe one day, but much too painful to consider at the time.

The house and land, however, ceased to hold importance because Anna would not be there to share them with him. With no family left, he could not imagine living where he would be reminded constantly that the love of his life was gone.

Anna understood why Roby had stopped and stayed in Kentucky, and as difficult as it was for her to accept, how Roby remarried. Anna was not surprised that Roby spent most of his adult life proving to be the man of character she always knew he was.

Catching up on twenty-five years of Burke events for Roby was a flood of events that could have taken days to hear and months to process. Two days of Court testimony told Anna everything she needed to know for now. Still, Roby's missing years would not be simple for her to outline or for him to accept. Anna tried to make it concise and topical, sure there would be time for details later.

"The Porter's sheriff came here looking for you as often as they ordered him to – it was never pleasant. They didn't bother me because I always showed em' my skillet. I started keeping it by the door after a while."

Roby felt his heart want to burst hearing Anna's sense of humor again, and in that instant, twenty-five years of missing her hit him at once as tears.

"Robert was born in October and I named him after your father. I knew you would want that. He grew up wanting to be just like you until he got older. Something was bothering him before he became a deputy. I see now; he became Sheriff to find you."

"I struggled for a while with the taxes, but when I went to the courthouse one day to make a payment, I found that the tax was paid in full. I know Lewis did it although he never said so. He did it for so many of us. He told me you met on the trail and asked him to check on me now and again. He did. That's why I never gave up on you Roby. I knew you were looking out for me."

"Lewis married Amos's sister Adeline, finally, and I delivered their boy and girl. It wasn't long after that Amos and Lewis were ambushed by the revenue agents out of Caldwell County. They killed Amos right off. Lewis got away, but I had to dig three slugs out of him. He was in the hospital for only a day before he slipped away and returned to Dark Corners. He knew everyone there."

Hurting thru and thru, Roby knew how difficult it was for Lewis to lose his best friend Amos Ladd. Amos and Lewis didn't just grow up together; Amos was Lewis's brother-in-law - Adeline's brother. F a m i l y . Roby already knew the revenue agents were widely known in the Carolinas as scoundrels and outlaws themselves. They would ambush a man without so much as a "you're under arrest."

"I got my medical practice soon after Father died. Mother died only a week later. The house and property are still there, but I live in the cabin. Robert keeps up the house and will probably move in when he does marry – He's sweet on Bill Padgett's girl. I don't exactly know why they haven't married yet. Our spring shower fell down in a storm, but it's still there. I like to go sometimes. The cabin is just like you left it Roby, waiting. For you..."

The air around Roby felt thick and made it hard to

breath, there was so much to say, but he was drowning in the mountain air and emotions of years of sorrow and happiness.

Anna was also quick to settle the biggest unanswered question hanging over the meeting. Of her own free will, she gave Roby up to his other wife, Sarah. It was not because she did not still love him, this man for whom she had waited twenty-five years, never accepting that Roby wouldn't return. It was that the most significant part of his adult life had been spent with the other woman. By all accounts, she needed him and his greatest obligation was to her. That day, Anna Martin would return to the still unfinished Martin cabin alone with her son.

Not entirely satisfied with the outcome of events, Robert released Roby from custody, relieved that the circumstances and actions that dictated the course of these events proved that his father was not the bad man that he had been afraid Roby would be.

Not yet satisfied with the idea of two wives, however, he was reluctant to let the matter go unresolved.

"You still have two wives. I should hold you in custody." Robert looked him in the eyes, not quite sure what exactly he was searching for.

Roby, still agonizing over the same problem, could only say, "I can't explain how difficult this is. I've never stopped loving your mother, but I have to return to Kentucky and take care of Sarah. She needs me, she, she needs me. Anna has you, Robert, and she's strong. She raised you well and gave you a strong name. I couldn't be happier for you both. It breaks my heart to leave, but I know Anna will be fine. Robert, I will see you both again."

Robert exhaled slowly, placing a tired hand on his forehead. All of this had been eating him up inside.

"It's nice, truly, to know that you are a good man. I lived my entire life terrified that I had murderer's blood in my veins. If I can thank you for anything, thank you for not being what I thought you were."

Roby grinned. "Most men would rather die than hear their son say those words."

"Well. You are not most men. And I, I'm not most sons."

Knowing that the road ahead of him was not as long as the road behind, Roby was resolute and determined he must make the best of each mile ahead. It was time for his return to Kentucky.

RESOURCES

BURKE COUNTY HISTORY

Zebulon Vance Estate

Civil War Historical

CRWedding Art Collection

PLWedding Graphic Arts

Cabins in the Laurel

Wikipedia

The Prince of Dark Corners

Ohio County, Ky Historical Society

All Photographs property of Author

Made in the USA
Monee, IL
05 September 2023

42173958R00063